We drift and dream,
again and again,
inside the dreams we create ...
inside the dream we are.

(excerpt from Hollow Gasp pg. 23)

Also, by Candice James

Print Books
10 PAK – 5;10 PAK–4; 10 PAK–3; 10 PAK–2;
10 PAK–1
A Potpourri of Paintings;
The Still Small Voice of Soul;
Spiritual Whispers; Atmospheres;
Blue Silence; Call of the Crow;
Imagination's Reverie; Short Shots 2;
The Depth of the Dance;
Behind the One-Way Mirror;
The Path of Loneliness
Rithimus Aeternam; The Water Poems;
Short Shots; City of Dreams;
Merging Dimensions; The 13th Cusp;
Colors of India; Purple Haze;
A Silence of Echoes; Shorelines; Ekphrasticism;
Midnight Embers; Bridges and Clouds;
Inner Heart, a Journey; A Split in the Water

10 FREE e-books
www.ebooks.net/poetry/Abstrusion
Abstrusion; Wonderland; Fract & Flect;
Year of Divine Madness; 60 Haiku;
Midnight Shootout; Naked Leavings
The Rising; CJ Poetry & Paintings;

https://www.everand.com/author/572119332/Candice-James

Transitioning

Candice James

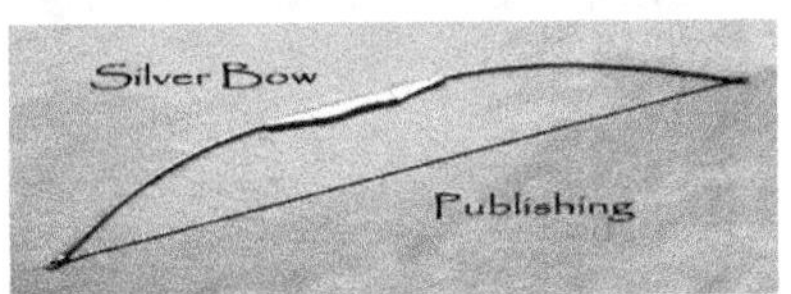

Box 5 – 720 – 6th Street,
New Westminster, BC
V3C 3C5   CANADA

Title: Transitioning
Author: Candice James
Cover Painting: "Sailing Into Sundown" by Candice James
Layout/Design: Candice James
Editing: Candice James

ISBN: 9781774033913
ISBN: 9781774033920
© 2025 Silver Bow Publishing

Library and Archives Canada Cataloguing in Publication Title: Transitioning / Candice James. Other titles: Transitioning (Compilation) Names: James, Candice, 1948- author. Identifiers: Canadiana (print) 20250310341 | Canadiana (ebook) 20250311674 | ISBN 9781774033913 (softcover) | ISBN 9781774033920 (Kindle) Subjects: LCGFT: Poetry. Classification: LCC PS8569.A429 T73 2025 | DDC C811/.54—dc23

CONTENTS

FOREWORD

Time, ah yes, precious time changes everything including our perspective.

Looking back, when I was 9 or 10 years old, I thought my grandmother was really old. Today, I'm almost 30 years older than she was at that time in my life ... and I don't feel as old right now as I thought her to be then. In our young days we don't think about getting old or death,

Now as I have entered what I think of as the last chapters of my life, I think about death and dying often. Some days I really think on it and feel it must be closing in on me. Other days it seems like it is not closing in, but just somewhere out there around the bend waiting patiently to come and collect me for the final journey home.

As I have aged, I find myself thinking on the past and I miss those dear ones that are no longer in my life more and more with each passing day. So many times, I feel them near even though they are long gone from this earthly plane. In my poem "The Gap Between Pulse Beats" I describe what I think death is like.

My hope is that this collection of poetry will soothe the aching heart for those that grieve and will calm the fears one may have about death being the end of everything. The finality of all. It is not the final destruction of our being. It is just a transitioning of flesh to spirit. We are not simply flesh and blood. We are souls inhabiting a body and death is just the burning off of the body from the soul; the separation of spirit from flesh. When we reach "the end" as we think of it on this earthly plane, we will realize that we are still the essence of ourselves and time is only an illusion and does not exist in the reality of the all.

So, rest easy, death is not the final frontier ... it is simply the doorway to the wonderful world of spirit. A reunion with *"Those Gone Before"* where this is no *"Aging"* and we *"Transition"* to *"Pure Spirit"*.

Death is not the end. It is just the beginning!

~ Candice James, Poet Laureate Emerita,
City of New Westminster, BC CANADA

Behind The One Way Mirror

They Live. They do live on,
in that other hazy dimension,
just beyond our reach.

They walk. They still walk
the canyons of our minds,
turning memories on and off,
in cinematic film clips of days
past, present and future.

They dance to their own rhythm.
Feathers brushing against our being,
echoing... *'Remember me.'*
        'Remember me.'

They breathe
their presence into our souls
to fill the empty space
they left in us when they left us.

AND We live. We do live on
behind this one-way mirror,
just beyond their reach,
        Waiting ...
        Waiting ...
for the mirror to shatter.

Remains Of The Day

So many years have passed
since I've heard your voice,
but sometimes, I swear
I hear you calling my name ...
in soft velvet whispers.

There are moments
I swear I feel your presence.

A fine, filmy residue
of those moments permeates
the remains of the day,
then gives way
to the fine, hazy residue
of your essence.

Time and time again,
I linger in the past
holding onto your memory
and... the remains of the day

Mother

After I kissed your cheek
rivers of aching pain flowed
into my wrist and fingers.

So many years together
and yet, so much time apart.
And now you've flown away forever,
a beautiful bird
leaving me behind.

Now, a new kind of lonely,
      Emptier.

Not a day or night will pass by
when I don't think of you.
Not a smile or a tear will appear
without some image of you in it.
You'll always reflect in me
like a deeply rooted diamond
dusted and powdered
with the sweet, salty, sugar
of yesterday's dreams.

And now, I am orphaned;
but the mother and child reunion
is only a motion away ...
      Only a motion away.

Spirit Mood And Tone

There is a spirit mood and tone
in the smooth of this evening.
A hazy remembering of things:
people and places
and those passed on.

There is a spirit mood and tone tonight
invading my being on every level.

Although you're gone
I still feel you,
so near, yet so far away,
and I shed a tear:

Remembering things forgotten.
Remembering you.
Remembering me.
Remembering us.

The Dream

You walk in dark shadows
at the edge of night
and softly climb into my dream.
And then the music plays.

There is a silken silence
as I search to find you,
knowing I can't.

I visualize you nearing.

As I grasp at your essence
you dissolve at my touch.

I cling to the silence
seeking solace,
trying desperately
to re-enter the dream,
knowing full well I can't.

Unexpected Guest

Turning the handle of sorrow,
raindrops fall softly
to blend with my tears.

A hard ache squeezes my heart.

When I am most lonely,
and I least expect relief,
        your spirit
wraps itself around me.

A soft velvet blanket,
warming the chill
left by your absence.

An unexpected guest,
But always, always
oh so welcome.

The Impermanence

In the distance
I see you walking toward me,
I open my eyes and your image fades.

I close my eyes for a minute
and see you looming larger
reaching out to me.
I open my eyes and your image fades.

I close my eyes and see you
standing beside me.
Close enough to touch,
but still, just out of reach.

Just out of reach.

So, *I open my eyes,*
and the dream dissolves,
and you fade from view ...
        into

   the impermanence
between here and there.

Every Day

Every day
I visit that little corner of my heart
I keep you in.

Every day
I shed a new tear
for an old memory,
embossed in gold,
that bears your name.

Every day
through life and death
I'll visit that little corner of my heart
I keep for only you.

A part of you
will always live in me ...
        always.

Fluid Silence

There is a fluidity to this silence,
a timeless tango,
dancing to the whisper of a familiar song:

There is a flexibility to this fluidity:
Spinning, within its own harness.
Dangling on a string.
Thinning to a thread.
Quickening to rope.
Encircling my thoughts

The same familiar song.
The same timeless face.

Always I waltz with you
through those lost hours
in the fluid silence
just beyond the veil.

Just A Dream

All our days are a dream
unravelling at its tattered seam,

We are shadows in a dream.
We're half awake but still asleep.

The echo of a midnight gasp.

We watch the light of life elapse.
We see the dream we are collapse.

We stand unravelling at the seam
inside this dream within a dream.

All our days have been a dream ...
          just a dream
                    inside a dream.

Hollow Gasp

We are:
droplets of water,
the dust of stars,
the breath of angels.

We are:
flakes of snow, shards of ice.
pirouetting, dancing
in and out of time
in a never-ending pool of timelessness
locked inside the hollow gasp
of death's death,

We drift and dream,
again and again,
inside the dreams we create ...
inside the dream we are.

This Side Of Heaven

The inky sky spreads,
stains the windows of my soul.

The night slowly drowns
in the dissolving moments
of endless time.

I melt into myself,
this side of heaven's clock.

I stand in the clutch
of a relentless rain.
knowing, deep in my heart,
you're gone from this world ...
    and I'll never hold you again
        ... this side of heaven.

Beyond The Shadow Of The Veil

Beyond the shadow of the veil
we will always be,
hand in hand beneath the sun
together flowing free.

Present, future falling fast,
into living moments past,
we'll live inside each other's breath
where there's no never-ending death
Where all roads lead to love,
by grace of God above.

And we will love each other more.
'Twill be again as 'twas before.
No separation will exist.
Love so strong it cannot twist
but strong enough to bend.
My loved one and my friend
from time's inception to the end
beyond the shadow of the veil

A Hint Of Perfume

After your death
there was nothing left of you
for the longest while.

I imagined the sound of your voice
calling out my name
from somewhere far, far away.

Years later, alone in an empty room,
I would sometimes smell
a hint of your perfume:
Immediate. Pungent.
I would turn and scan the room
for a hint of you
but, alas, I was still alone.

As years pass by,
alone in an empty room,
many times I suddenly smell
the scent of your perfume.
 I still turn and scan the room
        for some trace of you
               but I am alone.

I know you're not there,
but I've come to realize ...
                    you are.

The Veil

There was an ambiance to the evening.
    An atmosphere.
    A thinly veiled succor,
    that passed s l o w l y
    over the lips of the night.

A summer rain fell from a pale blue sky
as the wind grooved to the surreal
        u
    b   m
    p

           and grind
        of the raindrops.

There was an ambiance to the evening,
    thick with your imagined whispers
      and misty touch.

    ... I almost felt you through the veil.

This Slight Rapture

There always remains
at least one left-over spark
        or ember
to light the darkest night

  and there's always
  one left-over memory
to soothe a broken heart,

        I stand,
romancing the hands of time.

Wrapped in my solitude,
and dancing in the rapture
        of a coveted tear,
I feel your breath on my cheek
        momentarily.

Always there remains
a hint of your after shave,
and an image of you in my mind,
softly caressing
this slight rapture.

A Wisp Of Haze

I heard a weary voice inside my head.
A wisp of haze and then your body rose.
Magnificence shone on the ghostly dead.
You stood obliviously in silver clothes.

You did not notice me as I stood there.
I tried to grasp your hand, but it dissolved.
You sat down in your favorite easy chair.
A wisp of haze and then the room revolved.

Old mem'ries flew around like mockingbirds
mimed old love songs from our yesterdays
I saw you move your lips in silent words
before you disappeared into the haze.

Tonight, I'll wait for you to reappear
inside the hardened edges of a tear.

The Clutch Of A Fading Song

Trapped in the clutch of a fading song
with notes and chords that don't belong,
I stand at the edge of a broken night
bathed in sorrow and moonlight,
searching for you and yesterday
and distant dreams so far away.

Another long night lingers on.
The music and the dancers gone.
They've disappeared into the dawn
       but I remain
       inside the rain
trapped in the clutch of a fading song

       ... without you.

Drifting Haze

All the days, a drifting haze.
The dimming of lights. Nondescript nights.
Years pass like fog, wet, waterlogged.

I wait here on my ship of dreams
tattered at the seams,
wishing on a distant star
and wondering where you are ...
wondering where you are.

Waiting for the drifting haze
to take its leave from my days
The shimmer of lights.
Glistening nights.
Tears fall from the sun
as the dream comes undone.

And then ...
I see you approaching.

The music begins.
You take my hand once again
and we dance in the ether
forever and ever amen.

The Strand

Yesterday we walked the beaches
of another place, another time.

Today, I am a statue
turned to stone, standing alone
far from the beaches we walked.

On days like this,
I try to envision your face,
but you've been gone so long
        your image is hazy.
I try to tap the days of old
and dance within their crease and fold,
but they escape me like a lost breath.

The windblown day is swept away.
A brittle silver moon rises
spilling zircons and rhinestones
onto the shadows on the shore
and the statue on the strand.

The day and the strand dissolve
        as if they never were.

        But I remain
    — standing alone —
    a statue on the strand ...
        turned to stone.

A Beautiful Butterfly

A butterfly followed me along the shoreline.
A beautiful butterfly of colorful design.
It started to flutter to and fro,
with every step, each stop and go.
Mostly drifting on my right-hand side
as I walked the shallows of the tide.

As the day grew weary and I traveled on
I thought that butterfly would be long gone.
But, alas, it steadfastly stayed at my side
as I walked the shallows of the tide.

I walked and I whispered to that butterfly
of memories and dreams and days gone by.
I was sure it was more than a mere insect.
It seemed to command my deepest respect.

And then it hit me out of the blue.
Perhaps it was Karma and someone I knew.
I began to hum a familiar song.
A hint of your essence sidled along.

A beautiful butterfly followed me home.
I knew you were here. I wasn't alone.
Now each day I walk along the shoreline,
my beautiful butterfly soft on my mind.

Empty ... Full

My heart is empty
behind its blood-smeared walls.

A pale ghost
walks the canyons of my mind,
whispers through my veins,
lives inside my heart.

Your voice whispers
in falling tears,
softer than the tears.

Today
my heart is empty,
yet still full ...
full of yesterday.

Always It's You

This quiet evening
wears a jagged teardrop
pinned to its breast.

There's an ache in my chest,
a tear in my eye
and a hazy familiar memory
        riding tall
through the dimly lit canyons
        of my mind.

        Always...
    always it's you.

One Heartbeat Away

I spy a lovely butterfly
with glistening wings, passing by.

I close my eyes and move through time,
through music, rhyme and pantomime.
I see you standing in the light
glowing in the dark of night.

You're only one heartbeat away.
I want to come, but I must stay.

And so, reality steps in,
I'm back inside time's Siamese twin.

You're only one heartbeat away.
I long to come, but I must stay.

One kiss and one embrace away.
I long to come ... but I must stay.

Wings Of Time And Tide

You are always with me
riding high behind my eyes
speaking in gentle whispers
only I can hear.

The sacred butterflies of heaven
fly seamlessly
through the gaze of my eyes
and gather in the shade of my heart.

I don't have to close my eyes
to see you.
You're indelibly imprinted
onto my being.

You're always with me
riding high behind my eyes
on the wings of time and tide.

A Mellow Monet Work Of Art

A glimpse of steel, a flash of train
silent on an endless track,
and oh, that I could ride again
the rails and not look back.

You still waltz across my mind,
a tender wistful melody,
and in those moments lost I find
the music brings you back to me.

And now the years have come and gone
since those days spent on the road
You've travelled light years from our song.
Now days are old and nights are cold.

But still, you waltz across my mind,
a mellow Monet work of art.
And in those moments lost I find
you laying soft upon my heart.

A mellow Monet work of art ...
you lay soft upon my heart.

The Funeral

I stand silently,
outside the reception hall.
Ashes to ashes. Dust to dust.

Death is all around.
Cold in the earth.
Warm, walking on the concrete.

You're gone never, yet forever.

We, the remaining, exchange:
Tears. Faces. Smiles. Embraces.
Compassionate words.

You, the departed, remain:
A footprint on life's water.
A ripple on the earth.
A whisper on the wind.
A tearstain on the ocean.
Forever in my soul — Indestructible!

You're gone never,
Yet ... forever.

Rest in peace
my darling.
The struggle is over.

Solace

So many autumns
come and gone,
shuffled into a fading sunset,
caught in the chill of winter's breath
and the eternal sorrow of my mind.

So many faces and voices
dimmed with the passage of time.
Acquaintances forgotten.
Lovers only slightly remembered.
        Save one.

I find solace
in the whisper of your name.
In the imagined touch of your fingertips.
In the seasons of yesterday
overlapping all my barren todays,
all my tomorrows,
all my sorrows.

Some Days

Some days
I am afraid to die.

On these days
I am more vigilant.
more aware, more careful,

Some days
I am not afraid to die.
On these days
I am more alive,
more extravagant.

Some days are jeweled beaches.
Some days are damp gray sandbars.

The days pass by in a daze.
The nights dissolve in a haze
but I still find solace in my maze...
            most days.

Down To The Sea

I go down to the sea
to the lonely sea
where I know I'll find you.

I walk as fresh paint
brushing against breeze and tide
onto the canvas of time.

I listen to the spill of the ocean
as it tries to get into my eyes,
my heart and my soul.

You're gone but you're here.
I'm here but I'm there.
The real is surreal
and the surreal is real.

I go down to the sea
to balance my heart and soul.
To balance the here and hereafter.

I go down to the sea,
to the lonely sea ...
where I always find you.

You Are Here

The gentle toss of the breeze
through my hair,
whispering kisses onto my cheek,
dries the tears in my eyes
as I picture you still here beside me.

Sweet Prince of time and tides,
you roll in gently
onto the shorelines of my mind.

I hold hands with your ghost most days.

I see you so clearly
sitting on my right.
It's unimaginable to think
you are not here,
so, it must be true...
    Somehow,
you really are here.

You are here
with me always.

There is no death.

The Dance Hall Of Forever

After the rending apart,
in the echoed atmosphere
                of the still,
            a branch breaks.

        De Profundis!

        A Rain drop falls.
    A melody whispers...
            and I wait
    for the music to start.

            I wait
    to dance with you again
    in the dance hall of forever...

The Aging Process

One day you'll understand
why my mind is somewhere else
when I seem to be looking through you,
or into the edges of the mirror or the walls.
Every day I walk a little slower,
laugh a little softer, ache a little more
and carry yesterday's kisses and wishes
in the fragile cradle of my heart.
My mind wanders deep inside old memories
and tears brim in my eyes much easier.
Even now, as I write these simple lines,
tears are sliding down my cheeks
and I know not why... I know not why.

I'm thinking more on old days, old friends,
and old loves gone but not forgotten.
Sometimes I can't recall their names
and their faces seem hazy and blurred,
but their words still echo in my heart.
Sometimes I close my eyes.
Dreaming awake, I see their faces,
hear their voices. fee; their warmth
amidst a glow of music playing softly.
and I imagine I'm dancing again.

I've come to realize
this is the aging process...
One day you'll understand.

Early Morning Haunting

Through the foggy lens
of an early morning haunting
the ghosts of summer,
windblown voices
and hazy dreams
still linger
in the blue shadows
of a dying star.

I watch the sun rise.
Ash to ember to flame.
I listen to the wind.
Silence to whispers
        to voices.

I'm alone, but not alone.

I walk with ghosts
in the blue shadows
of this early morning haunting ...
                haunted.

Passing Things

Sometimes I hear voices and noises
that nobody else hears
and I wonder if it's the other side
reaching out to gather me into their fold.

Sometimes I smell a waft of perfume
and I swear my mother is nearby.

Sometimes. I swear I glimpse a ghost,
a fading grey shadow
nudged into the corner of my eye.

And there are times
I recall a jigsaw puzzle memory
with a few missing pieces ...
or pieces that don't quite fit.

These are passing things,
passing fast,
then slowly fading away ...
                         as am I.

Unbound

I try to recapture
the lost, almost forgotten joys
of childhood days and ways.

I try to marry them
to an aging heart
and failing mind.

The pictures in the photo album
        have yellowed.
The glue has lost its stickiness.
The book of life has lost its bind:
        The pages, kidnapped,
            are imprisoned
    in the inner sanctum of my soul.

And I am becoming ...
        unbound.
                fading, fading ...
                    fading away.

Turned Inside Out
***(how I think it might feel when one is moving
into Alzheimer's abode)***
Wandering into Alzheimer's night
I'm fading away from reality's light.
      I've forgotten the words
      to your favourite song
and the lyrics to mine don't seem to belong.
I can't differentiate right from wrong.
Memories I cherished are lost and gone.

as my hands start to shake.
I can't recall when my bones didn't ache.
I look in the mirror and see a white streak
has replaced the black strands
of my widow's peak.

Then my mind wanders. My eyes glaze over.
I'm a child again running through clover.

But still there are things I barely remember.
and January's now a prolonged December.

These things I've learned
from my sojourn on earth:
There are 2 sides to everything:
each of great worth.
A whisper's the other side of a shout.
And today is just yesterday
turned inside out.

My Name
(how it also might feel in Alzheimer land)

Slipping in and out of consciousness
and this recurring dream,
I search for the missing objects I've lost
along with the letters of my name.

I travel the shadow of my soul
trying to unravel the pages
that used to be me.

I'm standing amidst my baggage,
without a destination
begging a passerby
to take my hand
and take me to the land of lost alphabets,
that I may find my missing letters
to know my name again
and know ... who I am.

The Forgetting

I forget things now a bit more frequently
followed by a hollow feeling of alarm.
BUT ... there is a comfort in the forgetting.

It wraps itself around me.

A warm blanket, a lullaby,
and for a moment I'm a baby again
in a flash of dream and sleep.
                then back to reality
    which seems a more unfamiliar fit
    with each passing day.

        The aging process
        needs the forgetting
        to prepare us
        to leave the familiar.

I forget things more and more,
        with each passing day,
        as I cling more and more
        to my warm blanket
                in the unfamiliar lullaby
                of my last chapter.

Water And Rain

I long to go down to the shore again:
to hear the water speak to the rain,
to see the seagulls fly on high,
to hear the sadness in their cry.

The tender years when I was young,
when rainbows 'round my shoulders hung.
Those sky-blue days of golden tears.
These sky-blue eyes long for those years.

The long and winding path grows pale.
The mast now hung with ragged sail
sits all alone on a desolate shore
and I'll hear the seagulls nevermore.

The fleeting magic of youth is gone.
Life's music now a fading song.
The sky-blue skies have turned to gray
and soon my soul will fly away.

The days of life are beginning to fade,
an age-old stain on invisible suede.
And I long to go down to the shore again
to hear the water speak to the rain ...

to hear the water speak to the rain.

Page Of Life

Moving across the face of the sky,
a paint brush and fingerprint
        began to write my epitaph.

It was later than I thought.
        I had been sleeping
        at peace in the bed of life
unaware of the rapid passing of time.

Drifting and dreaming
to the beat of my heart,
life flew by in a flurry of days.

As I looked up from my papers,
the ink was fading fast from the pages.

The finger writing my epitaph
        had disappeared
and the ink was almost dried
        on the last line.

I saw myself slipping and sliding
        stumbling and fading,
                fading
        from the page of life.

Inside The Thinning

Inside a thinned crowd of people,
we are insignificant figures,
hazing in and out,
encased in the capsule of life,
a captive of our flesh and breath.

In between life and death,
         we remain,
      aging, lessening,
         trapped ...
   inside the thinning
    until we dissolve
   into the here-after.

Faces, People And Places

Familiar faces
are becoming unrecognizable
            and unknown faces
                seem strangely familiar.

Then suddenly,
                someone steps out
from the wheel of transitional time
                and burns the blur off my haze.

So many faces,
                people and places,
                    all familiar strangers
sharing one thing in common with me:
                none of us know who I am.

Lost Water

Alone and afraid,
I cross each smile
with a tear.

Depression
are miles above me now.

I am the lost water
of a desert dream ...
   dying of thirst
searching for the me
   I have forgotten.

Phantom Dance

The sky is a dazzle of starlight.

A hard rain spills,
in punches and jabs,
onto hollowed out deerskin and bones
that decorate my barren house of stones.

The wind whirls and swirls,
hums and drums.

I am aware of many phantom voices
inside the citadel of my nights
where I dance with ghosts
inside a forgotten song.

Transitioning

In the barren courtyard of my mind,
sometimes I dance to remember.
Sometimes, I dance to forget.

It looks as if
I am dancing alone.
but always I dance with you.

There is a bittersweet haze
wrapping its arms around me
whispering in a seductive, raspy voice
*"You can stop dancing
anytime you want
but you can never leave."*

Day by day and night after night
the dance lasts longer and longer.
Day turns into night.
Night turns into oblivion .

Through the haze,

I hear my phone ringing.
It just keeps on ringing and ringing
but I can't answer it.

I'm lost in the dance ...
transitioning.

December Heart

Through a crack in December's air
a winter song claws its way into my heart
and my night coils cold.

An ice-clad moon sink
behind the clouds in my eyes
in the dust-riddled gloom of the room.

Night coils colder and colder
around my December heart
inside this winter I can't escape.

The Gap Between Pulse Beats

I understand the gap between pulse beats.

It is the playground of ghosts
acting out dreams
in a one-dimensional landscape
beneath a quivering ocean of sky
that threatens to rain
in a blue stain of tears.

I understand the gap
between pulse beats.

A semi-death slowly stretching.

This space in between feels no different
than the echo of the pulse.

When it stretches to infinity
we will know the full embrace of death
and we will see there is no difference
between life and death
but simply a long-exhaled breath
and a gap in pulse beats that never ends.

This is the place where death dies

I understand the gap
between pulse beats.

The Winds of Perpetual Winter

When the dark sky curls its cold arms
around my stiff glass body
and tightens its embrace,
there is a shattering of unseen emotions
that speak in hieroglyphs and tongues.

My heart sighs and wrinkles
inside this glass body.
turning fast to crumbling shards.

I think about the earth spinning
slower every day
as the chains of death
draw tighter and tighter.

The transience of life never so evident
as when the winds of perpetual winter
slide in
on death's silent sleigh.

The Final Collapse

I'm an aging house of well-worn cards,
lost words, music and dreams,
moving into the final collapse,
coming apart at my ragged seams.

Death's bony finger
is wagging and beckoning,
calling me to my final reckoning.

My cards is torn and drawn.
I may not see another dawn.

Days grow short, so does my breath
in the cloyed clutch of impending death.

No More

Inside this cold, I hunker down:
Knowing the frost and ice approaches.
Knowing I am out of season,
past my *"best before date"*.

Dark, age-shadows on my face,
on my body, in my soul.
A reticent tear emerges,
flows, streaks and runs
into a wrinkled corner of my mouth.

Dark sky. Dark age.

I've grown old
inside this cold.
I turn to frost,
then ice,
and finally ...

I am ...
no more here.

I have crossed over.

Dust On the Doorstep

Memories ...
dust on the doorstep.

Hazy images,
stories swirling in the dust.

Stories I thought I might become.
burning brightly for a moment
then floating away
fading into the horizon.

The wind picks up speed
as the memories,
and my footprints
disappear ...
            like dust on the doorstep.

The Book Re-Opens

Tides, coming full
       yet waning and ebbing
         on fading shorelines.

Years, ages, faces, tears
trade spaces
reverse through each other
       spiralling the seasons,
    riding the rivers of life and death.

Windblown pages always moving,
          forward,
        backward,
    opening,
   closing, going past the end,
    back to the beginning.
through the pale iridescent dust of infinity.

We move through
the sparkling waters of eternity.
onto the wheel of karma and rebirth:

    A wink,
      a sanctified blink
        and the book re-opens.

Frost On The Grass

Yesterday dialogues whisper,
echoing in the silence,
ebbing and flowing softly
            through
disappearing star dusted nights
and cool crisp Spring mornings fading.

The season and I —
            disappearing ...
                  like frost on the grass.

A Distant Moaning

A distant moaning:
a silent song, a wordless rhyme,
drums whispering a broken lullaby beat.

The dead dance to their own music.
They dance to the songs only they can hear.

A string of pearls.
A chain of golden silver.
A pendant of burnt amber.
A candle of sage and sienna.

These are the things
that remind me of the dead.

These are the things
I will take to the dance
when I hear the distant moaning
and move slowly across
Time's river of tears
toward the dance of the dead.

A Matter of Punctuation

The birds of silence have landed
and taken up residence inside
the hours and minutes in my mind,
where the seconds keep winding down
past the limits of the metronome
that is my life.

A vague memory of a haunting song
plays like a rain dance
stolen from an indigenous dream.

I imagine the movements,
supple and static,
as I mime the names of the dead
for no reason at all except
to pay tribute and respect.

Tears punctuate my sentences
and form rivers in my story
as it heads toward the silence of the lake
that awaits just around the bend.
And suddenly there it is.
The flowing story of my life
and the lake that holds
all my punctuated sentences.

And there it is ...
The end.   Period.

The Understanding

We are knee-deep
in our own patterns of eternity.

Visible and invisible,
peeling hours like oranges,
sharing slices of time,
we are ghosts
filtering in and out of sky and soil.

Dreaming ... we're lying awake.
Awake ... we're inside the dream.

We are the vapid expectations
of our own personal poetry
filling page upon page
with fog and sunlight,
moonglow and stardust.

        Waist deep ...
we begin the understanding.

Dimensionalization (*a sonnet*)

Could we be but a structured form of paste?
A hologram believing we exist?
A spirit in a hybrid state of grace?
In actuality just moving mist?
Are we a portal to the other side?
Or mortals merely biding, chiding time?
Our spirit's breath can never be denied.
Its perfect rhythm interlaced with rhyme.
Our structured form continues changing
                                                face.

The body shed upon its final breath
as time and fate recycle inner space
revolving through the doors of life
                                and death.

Dimensionalization blurs our eyes
as soul moves from disguise to new
                                disguise.

Blue Mirror

We spend our hours in life's maze
on this side of the vast blue mirror.

With angels moving to our side,
the blue mirror beckons thee
to step onto its static tide
and sail the waters of God's Sea.

As we move in and through the blue
the mirror warms us to the bone.
We shed o<u>ur</u> flesh to walk with God.

       Nevermore
          to be alone.

Deep Inside The Dream

Cradled in the womb of time
I'm swaying on a quarter line.

And all the while a silent song
whispers as I travel on.

It seems a quite familiar tune;
reminds me of a night in June
when I was summer in the fall
so far removed from winter's call.

And now the days are losing light
as I hold hands with pending night.

Cradled in the womb of time
soliloquizing pantomime,
soul unraveling at the seam,
I am the dream ...
            inside the dream.

Heaven's Sea

I visualize your tears and smiles
hazing through the fog and rain.
And I would walk a hundred miles
if I could hold you once again.

Inside the harkening twilight
a lonely whisper beckons me:
To walk into the waiting light.
To sail with you on heaven's sea.

Amongst the lilacs where I lie
I offer them my wettest tears.
And all the while the fading sky
above me slowly disappears.

No need to walk a hundred miles
to hold you once again.
I taste your tears and feel your smiles
calling me into the rain.

I leave behind my written words,
my life song and a melody.
I shed my flesh to fly with birds
and sail with you on heaven's sea
for all eternity.

My Stories

In the crystal mirror of my mind
I watch the dream I am unfold.
I see my breath upon the air
writing stories to be told.

A distant bell is ringing,
a flock of angels singing.
I'm inside a living poem.
At last, I'm finally coming home.

I'm sailing on an ebbing tide
heading for the other side.
Again, I'll hold hands with my soul
when all my stories have been told.

Oblique

I am a being,
with no substance or essence.
A spirit:
seen but obscure,
flashing off and on,
walking with millions
yet walking alone always.

More here and less there.
More there and less here.
      Entwined in my karma
      far from my destiny.

This is the place of oblique lenses
I am here but can never arrive.
I am there but can never depart.

I have always been alive
sometimes in body
always in spirit.

I Am There

I've outgrown the skin I'm trapped in.
The world turns inside out.
Shapeshifting through the eye of a tear
I emerge in contrasts of myself.

Gray world turned black.
Eclipse of the eyes
lidding open to a distant monolith
slowly approaching, mirroring
pearls of hard moonlight and death,
wrapped in sacred breath
deep in the valley of blurred mirrors.

This is the afterlife.

... And I am there.

Remembering The Rain

I remember the rain:
The texture of its touch.
And the timbre of its voice.

The rain speaks
in many languages and tongues:
In a loud, raspy voice to some.
In soft, gentle whispers to others.

And then it stops
but its lips keep on moving.

Mine stop
and move no more.

When I am dead
remember me ...
remembering the rain.

AUTHOR PROFILE

Candice James is a poet, visual artist, singer/songwriter, musician, workshop facilitator and book reviewer She completed her 2nd three-year term as Poet Laureate of The City of New Westminster, BC CANADA in June 2016 and was appointed Poet Laureate Emerita in November 2016 by order of City Council. She is Founder of: Royal City Literary Arts Society; Fred Cogswell Award for Excellence in Poetry; Poetry In The Park; Poetry New Westminster; Poetic Justice, and Slam Central. She is Past President of the Federation of British Columbia Writers; Past Director of SpoCan and a full member of the League of Canadian Poets. Candice has judged the "Pat Lowther Memorial Award"; "Jessamy Stursberg -Youth Poet Award" and "Fred Cogswell Award for Excellence in Poetry. She received Pandora's Collective Citizenship Award and Chamber of Commerce Platinum award: the Bernie Legge Artist/Cultural award. She is the author of 39 books of poetry.

YouTube
https://www.youtube.com/channel/UC2EA5GcECIGYuF3o2KKHJFQ
FACEBOOK Poet Laureate Emerita Page
https://www.facebook.com/NWPoLoEmerita
FACEBOOK Artist Page
https://www.facebook.com/CandiceJamesArtist
FACEBOOK Musician Page
https://www.facebook.com/Candice-James-Songwriter-Bass-Guitarist156859754352277
Twitter:
@NWPoLoEmerita and   @candice23809987
Instagram
https://www.instagram.com/candice2926/

www.ingramcontent.com/pod-product-compliance
Lightning Source LLC
Chambersburg PA
CBHW070511170726
48291CB00008B/2710